As members of the
MAGIC ATTIC CLUB,
we promise to
be best friends,
share all of our adventures in the attic,
use our imaginations,
have lots of fun together,
and remember—the real magic is in us.

Alison *Keisha*

Heather *Megan*

Contents

Chapter
One

CHOOSING
SIDES

hand-lettered sign outside the school library read:

ACADEMIC BOWL
SIGN-UPS AND MEETING
3 P.M. TODAY

"Come on," said Heather, opening the door for her friends. Megan and Keisha hurried in to claim seats, but Alison hung back and Heather waited for her. "It'll be fun, Ali. Just like being on a TV game show. I promise."

Give it a chance, okay?"

"I'd rather be playing basketball."

"I know." Heather smiled sympathetically. If Alison hadn't needed a splint on her sprained finger, she would have been in the gym right now, doing what she loved.

"I'm no good at this trivia stuff," Alison said. "Whoever has me on their team is going to be sorry."

"I doubt it. You're going to be with us, remember? Come on. I think they're starting."

Mr. Valenti, the teacher in charge, was sending around a sign-up sheet. Alison and Heather quickly took seats beside Megan and Keisha.

"Everything okay?" Megan whispered.

"Fine," Heather said. "Ali's just nervous, that's all."

"Welcome to our first session of Academic Bowl." Mr. Valenti's smile seemed to reach out and greet each and every student. "We're going to have a lot of fun here. I promise." A few kids giggled nervously. "Thanks to our successful fall fund-raiser, this year's winning team will be going to the capital for the state championships."

"Cool!" Keisha's dark eyes gleamed at the prospect. Megan grinned at Heather and Alison. "All for one and one for all, right?"

"Definitely," Heather said, slapping Megan's palm.

Kids at the other tables were just as excited. Mr.

8

Valenti waited for them to settle down. "I've appointed five captains," he began. "Each of you will take turns choosing three other teammates. Let's mix it up a little, make some new friends, okay?"

What if he wants all four of us to be captains? Heather wondered. She glanced at Alison. "Don't worry, Ali," she whispered. "Mr. Valenti won't separate us. He's new. How could he even know we're all best friends?"

Alison nodded halfheartedly. "I hope you're right."

The teacher turned the overhead projector on and uncovered the names of two boys, Ben Lain and David Jennings, and three girls, Carrie Besmer, Jana Lovell, and Megan Ryder. Heather smiled at her friends. This was going to be perfect. They could all be on the same team, just as they'd planned.

Carrie's blond ponytail danced as she waved her hand. "Do we have to have boys on our team?" she asked when the teacher called on her.

"You might want to," Mr. Valenti said. "I'll be asking all kinds of questions, you know."

Carrie glanced about the room. There were lots of boys to choose from, but they were already inching their chairs closer to Ben and David.

"Would all the captains please come to the front of the room now, so we can begin?" Mr. Valenti rolled the projector to one side, making room. Megan stood beside him, and the two other girls squeezed in between Megan and the boys. "David," Mr. Valenti said, "let's start with you."

Heather wondered who Megan would choose first. Keisha, probably. Or maybe Alison. They'd been friends the longest. That was only fair.

Two boys left their chairs when their names were called and stood behind David and Ben. Jana chose her best friend. Next it was Carrie's turn.

"Hmmmmm." The tiny blond frowned as if she were doing a hard math problem. "I don't know. I can't decide."

Heather squirmed in her seat, wishing Carrie would hurry. She telegraphed Megan a silent plea. Pick me, Megan. Please pick me first. Were Keisha and Alison beaming Megan the same thought?

"Heather."

Heather turned to Alison and Keisha. The disappointment on her face was obvious. Keisha only shrugged. With a sigh, Heather found her feet at last and moved toward the front of the room.

"Oh, Heather," Carrie said, clutching Heather's arm, "I'm so glad I got you! We're going to win. I just know we are."

She was glad that Carrie had so much faith in her. "I-I hope you're right," Heather said, forcing a smile. She watched as first Keisha and then Alison took their place in line behind Megan. At the sight of all three of them grinning and squirming with anticipation, her own self-confidence leaked away like air from an old balloon.

Chapter Two

QUESTIONS AND ANSWERS

After all the teams had been chosen, Mr. Valenti called for a practice round. Carrie and Megan volunteered their groups for the demonstration. The eight students took their places at two tables up front, each equipped with four electric buzzers and lights.

Megan, Alison, Keisha, and Jamie, their fourth member, stood at one table. With a sigh, Heather joined Carrie's group at the other.

"This is like a quiz show," Mr. Valenti said. "I'll be

asking all kinds of questions, and you have to buzz in."
He continued explaining the rules.

Carrie nudged Heather. "We're counting on you," she
whispered, and Anna and Dawn, the other girls, nodded.

"Why me?"

"You're the only one who stands a chance against Megan."

Heather glanced at her eager friend. Already Megan's
hand was poised over her buzzer. A confident grin lit up her
face. Keisha and Alison stood on either side like bookends.

"Everyone ready?" the teacher asked. "Toss-up question."

Heather's stomach felt all fluttery. Why did everyone else look so calm?

"Come on, Heather," Carrie whispered. "Don't let us down now."

Suddenly, the room fell silent. All eyes were on Mr. Valenti. Heather pressed her lips together in fierce concentration.

The teacher cleared his throat. "What sport features a full-court press?"

Heather froze. Alison slapped her buzzer.

Mr. Valenti said, "You have ten seconds."

"Basketball," Alison blurted out.

"That's correct." The teacher put three points on the board for Megan's team. "Now for your bonus question."

Alison grinned at Heather and gave her a thumbs-up. At least *she's* feeling better about this, Heather thought.

Mr. Valenti continued. "What does a philatelist do? You have fifteen seconds."

Megan's team huddled, but it was clear that Megan was ready to answer. "Collects stamps," she said.

The teacher changed Megan's team score to ten. "Toss-up question."

"Come on, Heather," Carrie said. "Buzz in this time."

Why don't *you*? Heather thought.

"How many basic positions are there," Mr. Valenti

asked, "in classical ballet?"

"Oh! Oh!" Heather raised her hand, totally forgetting to press the buzzer.

Keisha remembered, though, and qualified for a bonus question with her answer: five.

Dumb, dumb, Heather chided herself.

"Bonus question," the teacher said. "What is the name of the riding competition that takes place in an arena and is sometimes referred to as 'ballet on horseback'?"

Keisha and Alison looked stumped. Jamie and Megan seemed to have ideas, though. At last Megan faced the teacher. "I don't know how to say it, but it's spelled d-r-e-s-s-a-g-e. 'Dress age', maybe?"

Mr. Valenti grinned. "Close enough. For future reference, it rhymes with 'massage'."

Heather looked at the score and sighed. Megan's team was up twenty to nothing. If Carrie and the others were depending on Heather, they were making a big mistake. She was terrible at this.

The questions continued: What is the fastest land animal? In what galaxy do we live? Where is the United Nations located? What

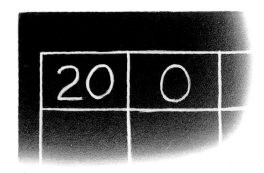

is Florida's nickname? How many colors are in a rainbow?

Even though Heather knew many of the answers, they dissolved on her tongue. Whatever confidence she'd had disappeared as well.

Carrie flashed her a hopeful smile. "Don't let Megan and those guys psych you out."

"They're best friends, you know," another teammate said. "Maybe she wants them to win."

"That's not true," Heather replied angrily. "I wouldn't do that."

The score was sixty to nothing in favor of Megan's team when the teacher finally said, "Well, you all get the idea. Our first competition next week is going to be heavy on geography, in case you want to study. Thank you, everyone. You may be seated. Are there any questions?"

What do you do about nerves? Heather wanted to ask. Instead, she followed her best friends back to their table.

"All right then," Mr. Valenti said. "We'll see you all next week, same time, same place."

On their way out of the library, Keisha nudged Heather and grinned. "What were you doing? Trying to go easy on us?" she teased. "You knew most of those. I know you did."

Heather only shrugged.

"Don't not try just because we're friends," said Megan

gently. "Even if you beat us, we'll still like you."

"I know." As the newest member of their group, Heather had always felt a little insecure. But now she realized that she finally believed them. Ever since the girls had tried on outfits in their neighbor's attic, gazed into the gilded mirror there, gone on an amazing adventure back to the 1930s, and formed the Magic Attic Club, they had been inseparable. Sharing her own adventures with them had only deepened the friendship.

"You said it'd be fun, remember?" said Alison. "And then you . . . What's going on, Heather?"

"I don't know." Heather shouldered her backpack and pulled her long dark hair free of the straps. She fell in step with the others as they headed toward home. "Maybe I should just quit and cheer you guys on instead."

Keisha shook her head. "If you feel that badly, maybe you should go directly to Ellie's attic. Do not pass go. Do not collect two hundred dollars."

Heather smiled. "Good idea, Keish."

"So, what sort of outfit are you in the mood for?" Megan asked.

"I don't know. Deciding is half the fun, isn't it?"

The others nodded enthusiastically. The roof of Ellie's white Victorian house rose like a distant mountain at the end of the street, and Heather's mood brightened. She'd check in at home, then go straight to Ellie's attic. What adventure awaited her today?

Chapter

Three

ALONE

Ellie's front window was open, and Heather could hear someone singing scales. But it didn't matter. Even though Ellie was busy with a student, Heather knew she was welcome to go inside, collect the key to the attic from the silver box on the entry hall table, and go upstairs.

And that's just what she did.

The attic was uncomfortably warm. Heather opened a few of the dormer windows. Soon a gentle breeze played through the room. Heaving open the huge steamer trunk,

Heather reached for an unfamiliar splash of red fabric. With a tug, she freed it from the other outfits. There seemed to be new ones every time she opened the trunk.

"A riding jacket!" she exclaimed. Folded inside it, she found a white blouse. "I wonder what I'd look like in these." She peeled off her T shirt and quickly tried them on. They definitely didn't look good with her pink shorts. "I can't go anywhere dressed like this," she muttered.

Another search through the trunk turned up riding breeches, black boots and hat, and a riding crop. Heather put all the clothes on and grinned. "Now that's more like it!"

A shiver of excitement raced through her as she approached the tall gilded mirror. Where would she go this time? Who would she meet? What would she do?

As she gazed approvingly at her reflection, something tickled her nose. Dust, maybe, stirred up by the fresh breeze. "Ah . . . ah . . . ah . . . choo!"

Heather found herself standing in the middle of a large, empty arena, with wooden rafters and narrow skylit windows overhead and a mixture of powdery dirt and sawdust underfoot. She blinked in amazement, letting her eyes adjust to the dim lighting. The air, rich and sweet with the smell of hay and horses, wrapped around her like a heavy blanket.

A large mirror on one wood-plank wall reflected the far end of the arena, which opened onto a paddock. Beyond that, Heather glimpsed a rolling green meadow dotted with horse-jumping fences. At the sight of them, her pulse quickened.

From somewhere to her right came a whinny. Turning toward the sound, she entered a stable. She made her way along the center aisle, looking from one side to the other. All the stalls were empty.

"Hello?" she called timidly. "Is anyone here?"

Nobody answered. On her other adventures, she was immediately greeted by people who seemed to know her. This time, eerily, she was alone.

She peeked into the tack room. Despite the heat, her arms erupted in goose bumps. Why did the assortment of bridles, saddles, and grooming supplies seem so familiar? She even knew which bits were

gentle—they were called snaffles—and which ones were more severe. I must be remembering something I read, Heather thought. The only horse I've ever ridden before was on a merry-go-round!

Just then a red tabby kitten shot out from behind a barrel of carrots and into the stable, tripping over Heather's feet. As she scooped him up, she noticed a large blackboard on one wall. Bold chalk letters said THISTLE DOWNS RIDING SCHOOL EXHIBITION DAY SCHEDULE. Below the heading was a list of late-afternoon times for various events—dressage, musical freestyle, cross-country, and stadium jumping. Dressage, Heather thought, like in the Academic Bowl question. In pink chalk, at the bottom of the board, someone had written: REMEMBER, APPEARANCE COUNTS! DON'T FORGET TO GROOM YOUR HORSE!

"Stadium jumping! Cool!" Heather nuzzled the kitten. "My horse must be around here somewhere," she said. "I think I hear him calling me."

She continued toward the open doorway at the other end of the stable, wondering whether she might have imagined the whinny. With a sigh, she set the squirmy kitten down. When she straightened up, she came face to muzzle with a sad-eyed bay.

"Omigosh!" Heather gasped. "Where did you come from, boy?" The horse shied away into the shadows of his stall, and she wondered who was more startled, she or the horse. A carved wooden sign mounted on the half-door said ADAGIO. "Is that your name?" She repeated the word softly to herself. At last the horse ventured closer. "Easy, boy. Good, Adagio."

A small white star peeked from beneath his dark forelock. Heather touched it gently, then patted the velvety softness around his nostrils. Adagio's dark eyes met hers, then without warning he sneezed into her hand, tossed his head, and turned away.

"Eeew!" Heather made a face and looked about for something besides her pants to wipe her palm on. "You didn't have to spray me. I was only trying to make friends."

Retracing her steps to the tack room, she found a rag in the corner. What if she couldn't figure out what to do, or how to do it? A mirror on the wall reflected Heather's doubtful frown back at her. She looked about, then straightened her hat and shrugged. Adagio had to be the horse she was to ride in the exhibition; he was the only one in the stable. She supposed she'd better get busy grooming him . . . and gaining his trust.

She selected grooming tools and braiding supplies for Adagio's mane, surprised that she knew which ones to use. Then she picked up a couple of carrots and an apple from another barrel and returned to his stall. "Come here, boy," she said, extending a carrot over the gate. Adagio didn't budge. The shiny red apple she held

out didn't work, either. Heather made clicking noises, trying to lure him closer.

"Poor you. It's going to take more than food to make that dumb old horse do anything."

Heather jumped, dropping the apple. She turned to see a tiny redhead whose eyes reminded her of Carrie's. The girl was dressed in riding boots, jeans, and a halter top. A frizzy ponytail exploded like fireworks behind her head.

"Hi, I'm Lynette."

As Heather introduced herself, she tried not to let the girl's comment worry her. Lynette obviously knew her way around, and she probably knew the horses pretty well. Still, Adagio couldn't be that bad. Otherwise, why would the riding school keep him around?

"You seen my helmet anywhere?"

"Your helmet?" Heather frowned.

"Oh, never mind. I've got another one in the clubhouse." Lynette blew out a breath that made her bangs dance. "Well, good luck. I'm glad I'm not you. See ya." She bounced away in the direction of the indoor arena.

"I don't care what she says." Heather waved the carrot under Adagio's nose again. "We'll show that Lynette girl, won't we, boy?" At last, as if he were doing her a great favor, he accepted the treat and turned his head away. His teeth crunched noisily as he watched Heather from the corner of his eye.

"Okay, Adagio, I'm coming in." Heather took a deep breath and entered his stall. "I'm just going to brush you. Easy now. Atta boy."

Though Adagio turned his flank to her, Heather continued to talk softly and finally began brushing. At least he stood there and didn't sidle off. Now that she had a chance to examine him, she recognized that he was some kind of Warmblood, one of those European horses that she'd seen on TV during the Olympics. They were considered the best breed for some special event, but she couldn't remember what it was. From his swayed back and swollen hocks, though, she supposed Lynette had been telling the truth. He was old. Very. Heather ran her hands over his legs, then patted his neck. "Poor Adagio," she cooed. "No wonder nobody wants to ride you. But don't you worry. I'll make you look good."

It took quite a while to comb and plait his mane. By the time she had wrapped white tape around each of the tiny, neat braids, Heather was beginning to believe her own words. The real question was, would Adagio let her make him look good on the course, too?

Heather lifted the saddle from the stall's half-wall and placed it on his back, smoothing the hair under the girth as she cinched it tight and made sure his skin was not pinched or caught. Then she slipped the bridle over his head and adjusted it. Adagio eyed her suspiciously.

"It's okay. I'm not going to hurt you." At last she led him out of his stall. "Come on, boy. We've got some jumps to clear."

But as she approached the stable doorway, a red-lettered sign above it caught her eye. FOR INSURANCE REASONS, ALL RIDERS ARE REQUIRED TO WEAR SAFETY HELMETS it stated. With a sinking heart, Heather touched her soft, black-brimmed hat. "Oh, great." She sighed. No way she was going to give up. But how was she to find a helmet?

Chapter

Four

WEARING
PINKS

H eather tried to remember
whether she'd seen
any riding helmets in the tack
room. Other than grooming
supplies and the few remaining
English saddles, bits, and bridles, all she recalled were
the carrots and apples, a tape player, and a box of cassettes
in one corner. Maybe by now Lynette has found her helmet,
Heather thought, and I could borrow her extra one.

She decided to head toward the stadium jumping course. If Lynette wasn't there, practicing for the exhibition, surely someone would be. Outside the stable, Heather mounted Adagio and took up the reins.

She tightened her back, squeezed with her legs, and kept a light, even contact with the horse's mouth to tell him to walk. She knew that these signals were called aids and was pleased that they came to her so naturally. Of course, she had read quite a few books about horses and had watched movies such as *National Velvet* and *The Black Stallion* more than once. Still, knowing just what to do in her adventures always awed her a little.

The sun, still low in the east, cast Heather's and Adagio's shadow across the gravel lane. At least it was early. Heather would have plenty of time to find a helmet, get to know Adagio, and practice before the exhibition. She could hardly wait to go flying over those fences as if Adagio had wings.

Impatient, she urged him along the path to the jumping course. As they approached a new barn, a man appeared in the doorway and waved.

Adagio halted without Heather's asking but did not shy as the man drew closer. "Good boy," Heather said, patting Adagio's neck. Instead of warming to her touch, though, the horse turned and blew air through his nostrils. It sounded as if he were giving her a raspberry.

"Don't take him personal now." The man mopped his brow with a red kerchief. "Gonna be another scorcher, looks like. You're new here. Name's Pete Sanborn, but you may as well call me Sandy. Everybody else does."

"Hi. I'm Heather Hardin."

"Glad to meet you." When Sandy smiled, his blue eyes almost disappeared amid his leathery wrinkles. "Fine job." He nodded approvingly at Adagio's braided mane. "Been a long time since this old schoolmaster's gotten fancied up for a show. Anything you need now?"

"Actually," Heather said, "I don't have a riding helmet. Is there a loaner?"

"Yeah, sure. Wait right here." He disappeared indoors and soon returned with one. Heather leaned down so he could adjust the strap. "I see you're wearing your pinks. Planning on doin' some jumpin', huh?"

"My pinks?" Heather frowned. She was sure she'd read that term somewhere . . .

Sandy tugged at the sleeve of her scarlet jacket.

"Oh. Yes. I forgot it was called that." A funny name, she thought, for something so thoroughly red.

"Well, good luck to you, missy. That's all I can say."

"Thank you," Heather said to be polite. But inside she was fuming. First Lynette and now Sandy! Just because

Adagio was old, it didn't mean he was worthless. Then again, maybe Sandy was referring to her!

"I'm headin' down to the stable now. But you just give old Sandy a holler if you need anything, hear?"

"I will," Heather said, "and thanks for the helmet."

Sandy ambled away on legs so bowed that Heather could see an oval of sunburnt grass between them. She supposed that's what came of a lifetime in the saddle. Had Sandy known Adagio when they were both young? He talked as if he might have.

Heather clucked her tongue and urged Adagio forward. "You must have been pretty spunky way back when, huh, boy?"

Adagio twitched his ears. She wished he could speak. Then he'd tell her himself what a schoolmaster was. Maybe Adagio was some kind of teacher-horse—really smart and in charge, just like the word sounded.

Over the crest of the grassy slope, riders were practicing their jumps. Seeing them made Heather a little nervous. And, no one was wearing pinks, which made Heather feel as conspicuous as a cardinal among sparrows. She hoped they would be changing their clothes later.

Just then a chestnut caught his hind hooves on the topmost bar, breaking apart one of the gates with a clatter. "That's not going to happen to us," Heather said to Adagio. Maybe if she pretended to be confident, the horse would believe she really was.

At the bottom of the incline, they passed a large rectangular ring. Twelve three-sided signs, each marked with a different letter, were placed at regular intervals around the outside. Heather wasn't sure what this area was used for. Thank goodness she and Adagio didn't have to worry about it.

"Let's trot, okay, boy?" She signaled him to quicken his pace. Adagio's swinging gait had plenty of bounce, and Heather was glad she knew how to avoid being jounced around in the saddle.

A young blond woman wearing a visor greeted her warmly. "So, have you two hit it off?"

Adagio shook his head.

"We're working on it," Heather replied.

The woman half smiled. "Good. Well, you keep working. By the way, the parents' club is putting out lunch in the clubhouse. I'll be around all day if you need me."

"Thanks." From the way the woman turned to direct

the other riders, Heather assumed she was an instructor. Heather would have to keep that in mind if she and Adagio didn't get comfortable with each other—and soon.

As they awaited their turn at the start of the jumping course, both Heather and Adagio swatted at mosquitoes. He pranced and shied, and Heather wondered whether his tail was more effective than her hand. At last the instructor waved them on.

"Okay, Adagio, here we go," she said, suddenly tense again. "I'm counting on you."

Heather signaled Adagio to approach at a canter. Her long hair flopped against her back. Sweat trickled down her temples from beneath the helmet. Could Adagio feel her nervousness?

The striped poles loomed larger. Beneath her, grass blurred. "Come on, Adagio," she said, bending over his neck. "And . . . up!"

But Adagio refused the jump. It was all Heather could do to keep from tumbling right over his head. He's just testing me, that's all, she told herself firmly. "Let's try it again, okay?"

As she turned him back toward the start of the course, Sandy's words rang in her ears: "Good luck to you, missy. That's all I can say." Heather grunted. She'd show him—and Lynette, too.

"Come on, boy." She leaned down and hugged his neck. "I've got faith in you," she whispered in his ear. "You can do this."

The instructor motioned her to go. Heather signaled Adagio forward, keeping her hands light. The rocking rhythm of his canter was like a drumbeat, urging them both on. The fence seemed to grow higher with each passing moment. Were they approaching too quickly?

Heather held her breath and closed her eyes. She was afraid to look. For an instant, she thought she was flying—until a sudden jerk brought her back to the truth. Adagio had turned away abruptly, avoiding the jump.

Tears gathered in her eyes as she slid from the saddle to the ground and leaned her head against his neck. "What is it, boy? Don't you believe you can do it, either?"

C h a p t e r

Five

OUT OF TIME

Try as she might, Heather could not persuade Adagio even to attempt any of the jumps. And it didn't help matters a bit when Lynette cantered past, flinging a smirking what-did-I-tell-you look over her shoulder. "Am I doing something wrong?" Heather asked the instructor at last. "What's the secret?"

"Teamwork." The woman winked. "Take some time to discover his strengths."

"Right," Heather said, trying not to sound skeptical. If

Adagio's strength wasn't jumping, then what was Heather doing here, dressed like this? She wondered whether she should just concentrate on getting to know—and enjoy—Adagio rather than on making him perform. She'd been so eager to try the jumps that she hadn't even warmed him up. Maybe she was taking things too fast.

With a cluck of her tongue, she signaled Adagio away from the jumping course and trotted toward the empty practice ring with the letters mounted around it. At least no one was there to make fun of her.

As they entered the carefully raked arena, Adagio's posture seemed to change. The way he tucked his haunches under him reminded Heather of her own stance at the *barre* when she did *pliés*. Was she imagining things, or was his gait really lighter and more dancelike? Despite the blasting heat, Heather shivered. "Are you trying to tell me something, boy?"

She continued to work Adagio in the ring, encouraging him softly. Instead of ignoring her aids, Adagio responded to the signals with surprising spirit. Unlike before, the horse seemed eager to please, responding to her gentlest touch. Soon they were tracing figure eights in the dust. Heather felt as if she were sewn to the saddle, as if she and Adagio were one. Sweat made growing dark swirls along his shoulders.

"I guess maybe we should rest," Heather said. She hated to stop, but another rider was waiting to use the ring. Heather halted Adagio in the shade of a huge oak tree and turned their faces into the breeze.

She wasn't in a hurry to get back to the stable, and Adagio seemed content to rest there, too. Curious, Heather eyed the rider who had entered the practice area. This woman, unlike the others, was wearing a black jacket, and her breeches were similar to Heather's. Instead of a short riding crop, she carried a long one with a kind of whip at one end. Heather watched, fascinated, as the woman and her horse traced forms in the powdery dirt. Had she and Adagio looked so elegant?

One of the Academic Bowl questions popped into her mind. "Adagio, is that what they call 'dressage'?"

Adagio nickered softly. Heather stroked his neck and continued to watch the horse and rider. Now that was teamwork! At last, reluctantly, she turned Adagio toward the stable.

Sharp, quick notes from a hauntingly familiar piece

of classical music wafted toward her from the indoor arena. Heather recognized it at once. How surprising it was to hear "The Dance of the Sugar Plum Fairy" from *The Nutcracker* in this place!

Adagio's ears pricked up and he raised his head and rounded his neck. Suddenly he began moving in a shortened, lofty trot, tucking his hindquarters more firmly under him and raising his hooves proudly. The joyful way in which he moved was contagious. Heather felt wonderful as the tension eased out of her muscles. "Is this what you love to do, boy?" she asked.

An image of dancing white horses came to her in a rush. It was from a Disney movie she'd once seen about some elegant Lipizzäners, horses that were specially trained in the Spanish Riding School of Vienna. Could Adagio have received that kind of training, too?

Adagio moved regally with the music until Sandy called out from the stable and he halted at Heather's command. "You've still got it in you, haven't you?" Sandy asked as he patted Adagio's neck, then added, "Wasn't that one beautiful passage?" He pronounced it pa-SAWJ, accenting the last syllable.

Heather had never heard that word before. But it sounded as splendid as Adagio's movements. She nodded enthusiastically and rubbed the horse's shoulder.

"It's like he knows the music, isn't it?" she asked.

"Horses never forget their training, you know, and this fellow went right up to international-level dressage in his day," Sandy said. "Takes a special rider, though, to bring it out of him anymore."

Heather blushed. "I don't know how special I am, but I'm beginning to see that Adagio sure is!"

"Well, missy, all I know is not many students get to ride a schoolmaster. They'd ruin him sure as shootin'."

"I don't understand," Heather said.

"This old horse knows the difference between this touch"—he placed one finger lightly on her wrist—"and this." He touched her again, but Heather could barely feel the difference. "If you put too many rough beginners on him, he won't respond to gentle anymore. And that'd be a shame, after all his training, wouldn't it?"

"It sure would." A crazy idea raced round and round in Heather's mind. Maybe she and Adagio could do an exhibition to "The Dance of the Sugar Plum Fairy." The music obviously still touched something deep inside him, and Heather loved it, too. Hadn't the blackboard listed an event called musical freestyle? "That music," Heather began, "was it on the radio or . . ."

Sandy shook his head. "We got plenty others on tape, too. You looking to ride a kur?"

"A what?" Heather asked.

"A kur. In dressage. You know, a musical freestyle."

"I'd like to," Heather replied, "only . . ." she hesitated. She seemed to have found Adagio's strengths, but she still wasn't sure what hers were. Somehow—so far, anyway—she'd known all the right cues to give Adagio. No wonder Sandy assumed she was an accomplished dressage rider, even though she hadn't known some of the technical terms. But what would he think if she confessed that she didn't know the first thing about musical freestyle? He might not even let her ride Adagio. If she could get enough pointers from other riders, maybe she'd be able to figure out a simple routine.

"Somethin' wrong?" Sandy asked. His white eyebrows ran together in a frown.

"No, it's just . . . how much time do I have before the exhibition?" Heather asked at last.

Sandy fished an old watch on a chain out of his pocket and snapped the case open. "All day, practically. But you'll have no horse left if you work him nonstop."

45

Heather dropped her gaze and nodded. She'd been selfish, thinking only of showing Adagio off before she lost her own nerve. She wondered how long Adagio would need to rest up. Would there be enough time to get the information she needed, make up a routine, and practice before the exhibition?

Chapter Six

HEATHER'S TURN

The morning heat in the stable pressed close around Heather as she unsaddled Adagio, checked his water, and offered him another carrot. Finally, she took her helmet off and shook her hair back.

"May as well take those pinks off, too," Sandy said, swiping his brow again with his kerchief.

"But shouldn't I wear—"

"Don't worry about it. Scorcher like today, you won't be needin' a jacket—scarlet, black, or blue. Hang it in the tack room, why don't you? And go get yourself a drink. We don't want you keelin' over on us." Sandy started off toward the paddock.

Without knowing quite what she intended to do or say, Heather found herself tagging after him. "Um, Sandy?"

He jumped at the sound of her voice. "Lordy! I thought you were—"

"I'm sorry," Heather said. "I didn't mean to startle you. It's just that . . . before—remember?—you said if I needed anything? And I . . ." She broke off, realizing how little sense she was making. "It's just that I've never done musical freestyle before," she blurted, "and I don't have much time to figure out what to do."

Sandy was smiling at her. "Tell you what. Go fetch that cassette you like and meet me up at the clubhouse. Get yourself a soda from the fridge. We'll work 'er out on paper, and then I'll talk you through it with Adagio in the practice ring."

Heather could have hugged him. "Thanks, Sandy. You're a lifesaver!"

Heather tried to memorize the routine while she ate lunch in the clubhouse. But the other kids were goofing around, making it hard to concentrate—especially when some of their jokes were about her and "Old Age-io." At last, grabbing an apple and what was left of her sandwich, she headed for Adagio's stall.

He whinnied as she approached.

"Don't tell me you missed me!" Heather grinned. The standoffish horse was starting to grow on

her. "Here. Want part of my apple?" She took a couple of quick bites, then gave him the rest. Adagio chomped it with gusto. "Want to hear the routine Sandy wrote for us?"

Adagio's ears turned toward Heather. She tried to recite the sequence of steps from memory, and was delighted that she only had to peek once at the paper.

"Guess maybe I better get you saddled up again," Heather said when Sandy came in.

"Might want to give him a massage first," Sandy suggested. "It'll supple his neck up some. But wait to put the bit in until you get him to yawn. You know how tough it is to make a horse take it."

Heather hesitated, unsure what to do. But once she entered the stall and laid her hands on Adagio's neck, to her surprise she began working his muscles as if she were an expert. At last Adagio yawned, and she slipped the bit and bridle on. Then she saddled him and headed for

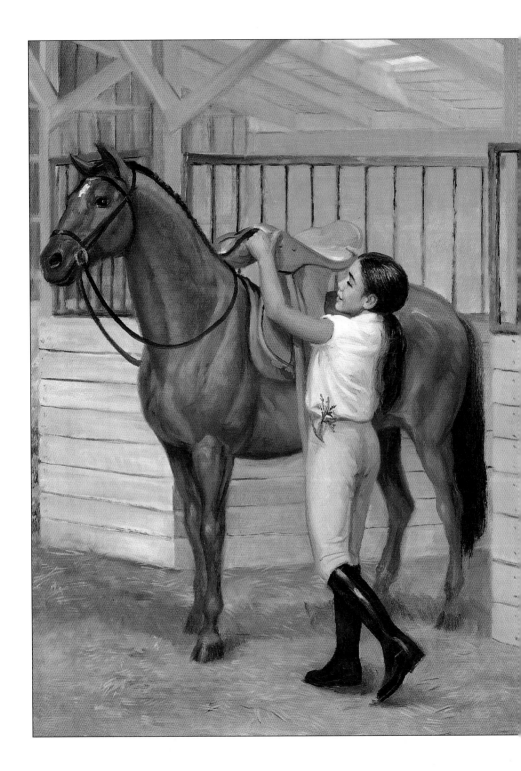

the practice dressage ring near the stable.

"All righty. Enter at A." Sandy waved the notes at her from his position at marker E, halfway up the long side. "Let's try it first without the music."

Heather nodded and listened for his cues.

"Enter collected canter," Sandy called. "X halt. Salute. Proceed at a collected trot, track left, change rein across the diagonal. Yeah, yeah."

Heather couldn't believe that she actually understood what he was saying and could tell Adagio what to do using only her legs and back. Amazingly, the old horse responded as if they'd been working together for months.

When Sandy at last played "The Sugar Plum Fairy," Adagio moved with new ease and bounce. It was as if performing had made him young again. Maybe he'd never been a jumper, Heather thought, or maybe he just knew he wasn't up to it anymore. One thing was clear: Adagio seemed confident in what he was still good at.

After the final halt and salute, Heather leaned forward and hugged him. "You are the smartest horse in the whole world," she whispered in his ear. "Just wait until those other riders see what we can do!"

Adagio twitched his ears, stamped his hooves, and flicked his tail.

"Better use some bug repellent. No telling what he'll do later on, when they're really bad." Sandy pointed out a spray bottle on the rail of the judges' stand. Then he hopped over the low chain fence that hung in scallops around the ring. His boots sent up little dust clouds as he ambled toward Heather and Adagio. "So what do you think, missy?" he asked. "You gonna remember the whole thing?"

"I hope so."

"Maybe you'd best do a few more run-throughs with Adagio, then study the paper awhile." Sandy handed back the written routine.

"Good idea. Thanks. You *are* going to come to the exhibition, aren't you?"

Sandy slapped at a mosquito. "I've got some work to do in the stable. But I'll be there. Wouldn't want to miss the look on Amy's face when she sees ol' Adagio come back to life."

Heather supposed Amy was one of the instructors. "Me neither," she said, then turned her attention to practicing the kur.

By the time the riders' parents and friends had gathered around the main dressage ring near the jumping course, their shadows were long and thin. Heather knew it was silly to search for familiar faces, but she

couldn't help wishing that
Alison, Megan, and Keisha
were there to cheer her on.

Three instructors took their
places in a wooden judges'
stand at the C marker opposite
the entrance. Though they
would be scoring the
dressage tests and musical freestyles,
the announcer said that since this was an exhibition, the
scores wouldn't count toward the riding school prizes.

Heather was grateful to be scheduled last. It gave her
more time to rehearse the routine in her mind. She was
lost in thought when Lynette sidled up on a gray mare.

"Too bad you had to take stale leftovers," she said
with a rueful glance at Adagio. "Guess you should have
got here earlier."

"Oh, I don't know about that," Heather replied vaguely.

"Well, I do." With that, Lynette dug her heels into her
horse and moved off.

Heather winced. That was exactly the kind of rider
Sandy had told her would ruin Adagio. How Heather
would love to see the look on her face when Adagio
pranced down the center of the ring!

Afraid she'd forget her own kur, Heather avoided

watching the other riders. Still, a doubt buzzed through her mind. Had she already forgotten something? By the time the team before her had entered the arena, Heather's stomach was turning flip-flops. Where was Sandy? What was taking him so long? Adagio tossed his head, swished his tail, stomped his feet.

"Easy, boy," she said. "What's the matter, huh?" She leaned over and patted his neck. It took several moments for her to realize that the announcer was calling her name.

Heather's heart beat fast as she urged Adagio toward the entrance at A. The familiar bursts of brass and string instruments blared from the speakers. Sandy's cues rang in her ears as she cantered in, halted in the center, and saluted the instructors. Out of the corner of her eye she spied the barn man coming down the hill. He was carrying something in his hand.

All at once, Adagio's ears went back and he skittered off his mark. The music kept playing, but it seemed to have no effect on Adagio's mood. Something was clearly annoying him. "Easy, boy." Heather urged him into a strong trot with her legs and back. "Settle down now."

He tossed his head, then halted abruptly, ignoring her aids. His weight rocked forward, and he kicked at nothing. Caught off balance, Heather grabbed for his mane. She missed.

Chapter

Seven

A REAL TEAM

O of!" Heather landed with a thud. Breathless, she gaped at Adagio, too stunned to move.

"Y'all right?" Sandy called from the edge of the crowd.

Gingerly, Heather patted herself down. "Nothing hurt but my pride," she said at last, borrowing the words from her father. With one swat, she nailed two mosquitoes on her cheek, then gathered herself up with as much grace as she could muster.

Adagio hadn't left her side, but he was still clearly

restless. He blinked at her, wide-eyed, then pawed the ground.

As Heather reached for the reins, a high-pitched hum filled her ears. She shook her head, but the buzzing persisted.

The blond instructor left the judges' stand and hurried toward her. "You sure you're all right?"

"Yes, I'm fine. It's just these dumb mosquitoes . . ." Heather's voice trailed off. All at once she realized what she'd forgotten to do. "Omigosh, Adagio! The bug spray! I'm sorry." She rubbed her face against his muzzle.

"Here, Amy." Sandy tossed the instructor a spray bottle. Heather stepped back while the woman spritzed Adagio from head to tail.

"There," Amy said with a smile. "Care to take it from the top?"

Adagio bobbed his head, and Heather laughed. "That goes for me, too!"

Heather remounted. Suddenly, her confidence seemed to flow away like water down a drain. Performing a kur was completely beyond her, especially in front of all these strangers. Adagio would know it, too. He'd balk just the way he had on the jumping course.

A Real Team

Heather looked at Adagio. His head was turned, and one big brown eye stared at her as he nickered softly. "You really think we can do this, boy?" she whispered. "Okay, here we go."

She squared her shoulders and began again. "Good boy," she whispered as Adagio changed directions on command, moving with the music into some fancy sideways footwork she'd learned was called a half-pass. As Adagio lengthened his trot, the beat of his gait became more pronounced. Heather nearly panicked again. What came next? Then Sandy's cue shot through her mind. Of course. The pirouette. Adagio circled around his two hind legs.

The rest of the ride clicked into place. From the fifteen flying changes at the canter to the regal piaffe where Adagio pranced in place for ten steps, Heather and her horse were finally a team.

As the last strains of music drifted away and Heather saluted the judges from the center of the ring, whistles and applause rose from the crowd. The three judges stood and returned her salute. Even Lynette, watching nearby, was cheering enthusiastically.

"We did it, Adagio!" Heather leaned forward and threw her arms around the horse's neck.

The announcer invited the dressage riders to join

Heather and Adagio in the ring. Heather was glad she'd decided to ride in her short sleeves. It was too hot and sticky to wear a jacket.

As the teachers presented ribbons to the riders, they had something good to say about each one's effort. The ponytailed instructor came to Heather last.

"Seeing you on Adagio," she said, "was like bringing my mother back to life. Mom rode him Grand Prix when I was your age. Nobody else has been able to bring out that wonderful piaffe of his." She handed Heather a blue ribbon. "If anyone deserves this, you sure do."

"Thank you," Heather said, "but Adagio is the real winner."

Heather wished she could make the walk back to the stable last forever. She knew she had to leave, but it was the last thing she wanted to do. She took her time removing Adagio's saddle, hosing him off, and rubbing him down. "There," Heather said with a sigh. "I guess that about does it."

Adagio nibbled at Heather's left hip pocket and she laughed. "You're right," she said, pulling out one last carrot. "I'd forgotten all about this, too."

He gobbled it greedily, then blew air through his lips, tickling Heather's palm.

"Silly boy." Heather giggled. She took a small red apple from the ledge and caressed the star on Adagio's forehead while he ate. Then, kissing the blue ribbon, she tacked it to his stall. "So you won't forget me, okay?" She hugged him and buried her face in his neck. Tears welled, threatening to spill over.

Adagio lowered his head and regarded her with wide, unblinking eyes.

"Don't look at me like that. I really do have to go,
boy." With a loud sniff, Heather pulled herself away.
"Bye, Adagio. I promise I'll never forget you."

With that, she dashed from his stall, collected her
jacket, and approached the mirror in the tack room.
She dabbed at her eyes. When she glanced again at
her reflection, she was in Ellie's bright attic and the
older woman was calling her name from downstairs.

"Oh, Heather dear," Ellie sang out. "Your father
is here."

Dad? He wasn't supposed to be home until
tomorrow. Hurriedly, Heather changed into her own
clothes and clattered downstairs. Her father and Ellie
were in the den. Heather raced to give him a hug.
"Daddy, what are you doing here? I thought you were
supposed to be in San Francisco."

"Schedule change. It's a lucky thing, because I've
been missing my girls."

"And we've been missing you, too." Heather grinned.

"Thought we'd have a D-D night, how about it?"

"Absolutely!" Heather quickly explained to Ellie
about the tradition of Dad-Daughter nights, when only
she and her father would go out for pizza and a special
movie. Jenna and Dad had their own outings.

"I'd say you're both lucky," said Ellie with a wink at

Heather. She rose from the antique sofa and escorted them to the door. "You *will* have an anchovy for me, won't you?"

Heather looked at her father. He was grimacing. "Um, maybe next time, Ellie," she said with a laugh.

Heather's unexpected outing with her father to Poppa Pepperoni's almost made up for having to leave Adagio. And though she was dying to tell her father all about her triumph at the riding school, she knew that he would never understand. Instead, over her second slice of double pepperoni, she told him about her disappointing Academic Bowl session earlier that day.

"The girls were counting on me," Heather said, "and I totally let them down. The first real round is next week, and I don't want that to happen again." She groaned at the thought. "Maybe I should just quit."

"Wouldn't that be letting your team down more?" her father asked gently. Heather said nothing. "You know," he continued, "if you ask me, it's an oxymoron to say a team depends on just one person. Ever heard of a one-person team?"

Heather loved the sound of that word, *oxymoron*, even though she didn't always remember what it meant. "You mean, it's not really a team unless everybody works together?"

A Real Team

"You got it, kiddo." With a napkin, her father dabbed at a greasy spot on Heather's cheek and smiled. "Everybody has strengths. A good team figures out a way to use them all."

Like her and Adagio, Heather thought. Once she'd learned to work with him, they'd done really well. No reason it shouldn't be the same with the Academic Bowl—especially now that she felt so much more sure of her own abilities.

Still, she couldn't help remembering how she'd frozen up at the bowl practice even though she'd known the answers. She mentioned this to her father.

"Well, it's no wonder," he said. "That's too much pressure, thinking everything depends on you. You're just one member of a team. Being confident is easier when you know you're doing your best, Heather, and believe that that's good enough."

"But the topic for next week is geography. Could you help me study for it while you're home?"

He gave her a look of amazement. "After all the places we've lived and all the routes I've shown you on maps? No way." Then he broke into the special grin that meant he'd been teasing. "Ease up, kiddo. Of course I'll help you bone up—even though you don't need it. This next session ought to be a cinch."

Chapter Eight

MISSING
ADAGIO

O ver the next week, Heather kept her adventure alive by talking about Adagio with Megan, Keisha, and Alison. She couldn't believe how much she missed him. At least her friends seemed to understand.

"Keep yourself busy," Alison advised. "That's what I'd do."

So Heather turned her thoughts to the upcoming competition. She spent her free time studying maps and old *National Geographics*. Carrie and the others had promised to study, too. Now, however, as they all gathered in the hall outside the library, Carrie, Anna, and Dawn looked as if they were coming unglued.

"Oh, Heather," Carrie said, "we've just got to do better than last time. Remember, we're counting on you."

"No pressure or anything. Sheesh." Heather shook her head. "Look. I'm counting on you guys, too. All we have to do is do our best and work together. Four heads are better than one any day, right?"

"I guess so," Carrie said, and the others nodded.

"Well, believe it," said Heather firmly. "Everybody's good at something."

"Dawn never seems to have any trouble in science," said Anna. Dawn's cheeks turned pink.

"I guess I know a lot about music and books," Carrie admitted. "Not to brag or anything."

Among the four of them, Heather thought, they ought to do pretty well with history, math, and geography, too.

"Then let the best team win," said Dawn.

Heather grinned.

Missing Adagio

Megan's group was on a roll. After beating David's team and Jana's team in record time, they finally squeaked past Ben's by only ten points. Now Heather, Carrie, Anna, and Dawn took their places at the buzzers.

"Remember," Heather whispered, "it's up to all of us. And our best is good enough."

"Toss-up question," Mr. Valenti said. "What capital city is named after our fourth president?"

Heather hit her button at the same time as Megan. Who would Mr. Valenti call on?

"Megan," the teacher said. Heather's stomach fell.

"Washington, D.C.," replied Megan confidently.

"No, it's Madison," blurted Heather, "in Wisconsin."

"That's correct." The teacher smiled at Heather.

"Didn't you say first president?" asked Megan.

Mr. Valenti shook his head. "Fourth. Sorry. And since it was pretty much a tie on buzzing in, I won't call that a 'steal'."

"Oh, goodie." Carrie giggled. "We get a bonus, then."

Megan shrugged good-naturedly.

"Bonus question. What is the lowest-pitched brass wind instrument?"

Carrie buzzed in without a moment's hesitation. "A tuba!" She flashed a thumbs-up at Heather.

Megan's team won the next toss-up, but they missed

the bonus. The next toss-up was easy: "Which war began
with a tea party?" Anna beat Keisha to the button. "The
American War of Independence," she said. "The
Revolutionary War." Dawn nailed the bonus question.

"See?" Heather whispered.
"Isn't this better than
last time?"

"I can almost see
that shiny capitol
dome already." Carrie
giggled again.

"Shhh!" one of
the others hissed softly.
"Don't jinx us."

"Toss-up question. How
many white stripes are on the American flag?"

Heather hesitated. It was easy enough to imagine the
flag flying from the pole in front of the school, but she
couldn't quite picture the red and white stripes separately.
The only other image that came to mind was the Betsy Ross
flag, with its circle of thirteen stars. She nearly blurted out
the word *thirteen*, but she knew that couldn't be right.

The other girls were whispering beside her, but she
was thinking so hard that she couldn't even tell which voice
was whose. "There are thirteen stripes altogether, aren't

there? Red and white minus red equals white, so thirteen minus . . ." Obviously that was Anna, the math whiz. The seconds were ticking away.

Heather's hand shot out and slapped the buzzer, and she looked at her teammates.

"Go ahead, Heather," Carrie whispered.

She still couldn't think of the answer. Oh, well, she might as well take a chance. "Uh, six?"

"Six it is!" Mr. Valenti laughed at the confused expression on everyone's faces.

"It's not seven?" Megan asked.

Mr. Valenti shook his head. "Red's on top and on the bottom, remember?"

Megan hit her forehead with her hand. "Very good, Heather." She doffed an imaginary cap and gave a little bow in Heather's direction.

Heather's cheeks went hot. She'd made a lucky guess on a simple question that happened to stump everyone, that was all. Still, she hadn't given up, and neither had her teammates. That definitely made this session a lot more fun than the last one. Win or lose, at least they all had the confidence to keep trying.

Only Alison knew that "tag'em out" was the answer to "What should the catcher do if the batter tips the ball on the third strike?" And Keisha replied that

69

the queen is the most powerful chess piece.

Back and forth the points went. It was clear that Heather and her group were giving Megan's team reason to worry.

"Well, well, well," Mr. Valenti said. "I can see we're going to need a tiebreaker. The team that wins this question is one step closer to taking that trip to the state championship."

Heather crossed her fingers. She'd be happy for Megan, Keisha, and Alison if their team got to go, of course. But she was sure glad her team had a chance, too.

The teacher cleared his throat. "Last toss-up question. What does *adagio* mean?"

Heather's hand flew to the buzzer with a will of its own.

"Yes, Heather?"

Her throat went suddenly dry. She'd meant to ask Sandy about the horse's name but never had. Her eyes wide with panic, Heather turned to Carrie. The tiny blond caught her hand and squeezed.

"I-I think it means 'slow in tempo'," Carrie replied.

"Correct, and congratulations!"

Carrie breathed a sigh of relief. "Thanks for letting me take that one, Heather."

Heather bit back the truth as the girls all hugged one another. Megan, Keisha, and Alison came over

and gave Heather hugs of their own.

"You did great," Megan said.

"We really worked as a team, didn't we?" Heather asked, still amazed at the results. After a few minutes, she and the other Magic Attic Club members finally picked up their backpacks and headed out of the library. "I don't believe how I choked on that last question about *adagio*, do you?"

"No wonder." Keisha grinned. "And only the Magic Attic Club will ever know why, right?"

"You got it, Keish," Alison said. "'Slow in tempo' is *not* what *adagio* means to us!"

Heather nodded and, knowing she would hold that other meaning in her heart forever, fell in step with her friends toward home.

Diary

Dear Diary,

When I ended up on Carrie's Academic Bowl team instead of Megan's, I was really bummed. I mean, there I was telling Alison we'd all be together, and who ends up being on a different team? Me! And it didn't help matters when Carrie and those guys kept saying everything depended on me.

I keep thinking about my adventure. I had no idea that by trying on that red jacket, I mean, those pinks, I'd end up doing dressage. I'd never even heard the word until the Academic Bowl practice session. If I hadn't really listened to Adagio, who knows how long I'd have kept trying to make him into a jumper!

Here's one interesting thing I found out from Sandy. You know the long tie on the blouse that one rider wore? It's called a stock tie. Wearing it is an important tradition. If a rider or horse gets hurt, it can be a tourniquet or bandage. Isn't that cool? I'm glad I didn't need to use it, though.

       Dad and I enjoyed our D-D night at Poppa Pepperoni's. I liked his oxymoron about a team not depending on only one person. I guess it made sense to Carrie and those guys, too, because we all worked together and managed to beat Megan's team. What a way to find out what adagio means. But at least hearing his name made me buzz in first!

               Luv,

                    Heather

Learn More About It

A SHORT HISTORY OF DRESSAGE

Dressage comes from the French word that means "training." Horses in ancient Greece were probably the first to be schooled in this tradition. Back then, trainers wanted horses to be obedient and dependable in war. Dressage taught them to perform unnatural moves, such as leaping about while their riders were dueling with swords. A well-aimed kick on command could surprise—or even take out—the rider's enemy.

These days, trainers still want to create perfect harmony between horse and rider. But now, dressage is something people do for fun or sport. The rider uses a bridle, a gentle bit with no restraints, and an English saddle that, unlike a Western one, has nothing to hold onto. She learns to signal her horse with very slight movements of her legs, back, and hands. Through patient repetition—instead of fear tactics—she teaches her horse to read her cues, or aids.

With years of training, the horse, like a dancer or a

gymnast, becomes stronger and more flexible. He can tell whether his rider wants him to walk, trot, canter, or halt—all without even hearing her voice. He knows when she wants him to lead with a different leg, turn in a circle, prance in place, or move sideways. People watching dressage—especially at the higher levels—find this display amazing. It seems as if the horse is reading the rider's mind!

Dressage competitions take place in a small (60 x 120 feet) or standard (60 x 180 feet) arena. Evenly spaced around the outside are signs with letters. These mark the points where riders start and finish the required movements and figures in their tests. Judges score the ride, movement by movement, on a scale of zero to ten. The horse and rider with the most points place first in their class.

Competitions are available for riders of all levels, from the beginner to Olympic-level Grand Prix Masters. In addition, most dressage events offer musical freestyle rides, also called kurs. In these, the rider selects her own music and creates a kind of ballet on horseback. Kurs are the only dressage events that are timed. They often involve just one horse and rider team, but sometimes they are performed with one or more teams. It takes a lot of practice to keep them all in time with the music.

Another type of competition that involves dressage is called combined training, or, at the Olympic level, eventing. Combined training grew out of the methods used by the military in the old days to select horses for its cavalry. These tests are designed to measure the strength, endurance, and athletic ability of both horse and rider. They usually have three to five phases of competition. Dressage is always performed first. It demonstrates whether the horse and rider are a well-disciplined team. The cross-country event features a course of permanent obstacles designed to show off the team's strength and stamina. Show jumping gates, on the other hand, break apart if the horse hits them. Speed and accuracy in this third event—especially after horse and rider have performed the exacting moves of dressage and the exhausting cross-country race—are proof of a winning combination.